Sharing Hanukkah

by Janet McDonnell
illustrated by Diana Magnuson

created by Wing Park Publishers

CHILDRENS PRESS®
CHICAGO

Library of Congress Cataloging-in-Publication Data

McDonnell, Janet, 1962-
    Sharing Hanukkah / by Janet McDonnell ; illustrated by Diana
Magnuson.
        p.   cm. — (Circle the year with holidays)
    "Created by Wing Park Publishers."
    Summary: Visiting his Jewish friend David, Michael hears the
story of Hanukkah, tastes latkes, watches the lighting of the
menorah, and plays a few games of dreidel.
    ISBN 0-516-00685-1
    [1. Hanukkah—Fiction. 2. Jews—Fiction.] I. Magnuson,
Diana, ill. II. Title. III. Series.
PZ7.M478436Sh   1993
[E]—dc20   93-13250
                                          CIP
                                          AC

Sharing Hanukkah

David and Michael are best friends. They live in the same apartment building. They ride the same school bus. They are in the same class. And after school they play together.

One afternoon, David knocked on Michael's door. "Hey," he said, "do you want to come up tonight and celebrate Hanukkah with my family?"

"What's Hanukkah?" Michael asked.

"It's a Jewish holiday. It's lots of fun. Ask your mom if you can come."

So Michael did. "Yes," said his mother. "But remember to say thank you."

"I will," said Michael.

When they got to David's apartment, Michael smelled something delicious cooking. David's family and relatives were all talking and laughing. The room was decorated with colorful streamers and a sign that said, "Happy Hanukkah!"

"Welcome, Michael!" said David's father.

"We're glad you could come. And you're just in time! We're about to light the menorah."

"That's the Hanukkah lamp," explained David. "Hanukkah lasts eight days. The first day we light one candle. Then each night we light one more candle. Tonight is the last night, so we'll light them all."

Everyone stopped talking. They gathered around the beautiful candlestick that had nine candles. "The one in the center is called the shamash," David told Michael. "It is the helper candle. We use it to light the other eight." David's father lit the shamash. Before he gave it to David so he could light the first candle,

the family said a prayer, giving thanks and praise to God. Michael watched as each person took a turn lighting a candle. When all were lit, David's family said another prayer. Then David's mother put the menorah in a window. "We want everyone to see it," she said.

Then she sat down at the piano. "Now let's sing a song," she said. David and his family joined in singing songs that Michael had never heard before. One of them began, "O Hanukkah, O Hanukkah, come light the menorah!"

After a few songs, David's mother said, "Grandpa, please come play the piano. I need to get back to my cooking!"

As David's grandpa began to play, Michael asked, "Why does Hanukkah last eight days?"

"You'll find out," said David. "On this night my grandpa always tells the story of Hanukkah."

Just then David's mother came out of the
kitchen with a big platter piled high with round,
golden patties. "It's latke time!" she said.

"Latkes are potato pancakes," David told
Michael. "We have them every Hanukkah.
They're good. You'll like them."

As it turned out, Michael did not just like latkes, he loved them! Every time David's mother asked Michael if he would like more, he said, "Yes, please," and everyone laughed.

"I think we have a new champion latke-eater," said David's grandmother.

When they finished eating, David's grandpa said, "Now it is time to remember the story of Hanukkah.

"Over 2,000 years ago, Jewish people in the land of Judea were ruled by a cruel king named Antiochus.

This king wanted to force the Jews to stop praying to their one God and instead pray to the gods that the king believed in. He believed there were many gods—a god of fire, a god of sea, and others.

"The king's men took over the Jewish Temple, which was a very important place to the Jews. The king's men put statues of their gods in the Temple. They made it a dirty and unholy place, a place where God's rules were not kept.

"Because many Jews were afraid of the king's

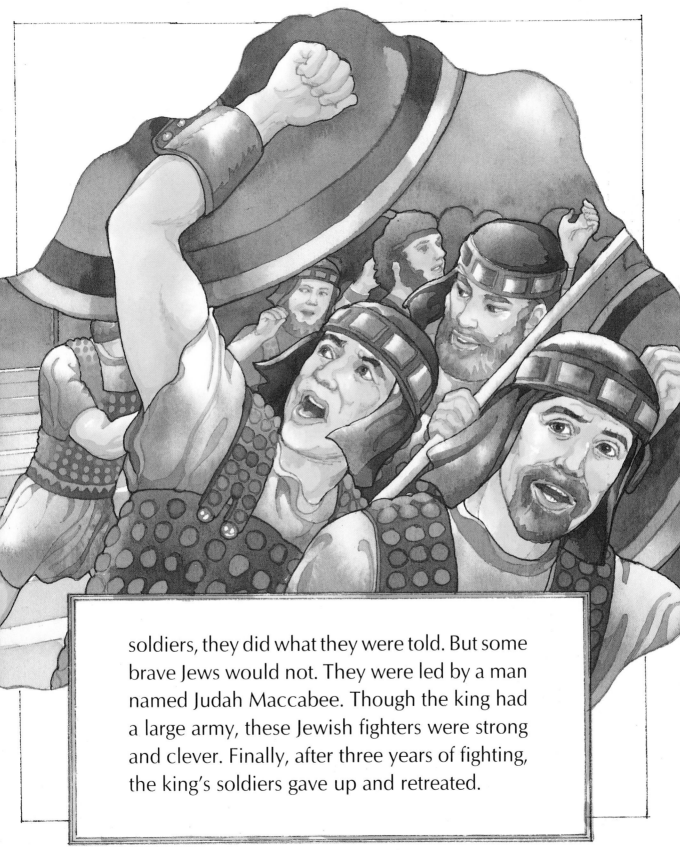

soldiers, they did what they were told. But some brave Jews would not. They were led by a man named Judah Maccabee. Though the king had a large army, these Jewish fighters were strong and clever. Finally, after three years of fighting, the king's soldiers gave up and retreated.

"The Jews were overjoyed! The Temple was theirs again! They got rid of the king's statues. They worked hard to clean the Temple and fix it up. They made it a holy place again, a place where God's rules were kept. And when they were done, they had a celebration and dedicated the Temple to God.

"The story has been passed down through the ages that there was only one small jar of oil with which to light the lamps for their celebration. They thought the oil was only enough to burn for one day. But to everyone's amazement, the oil lasted eight days."

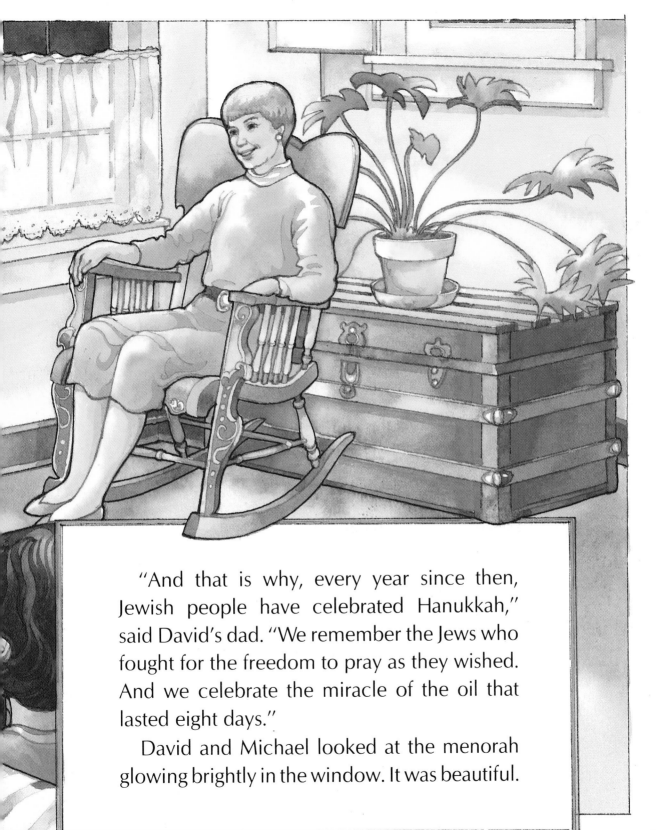

"And that is why, every year since then, Jewish people have celebrated Hanukkah," said David's dad. "We remember the Jews who fought for the freedom to pray as they wished. And we celebrate the miracle of the oil that lasted eight days."

David and Michael looked at the menorah glowing brightly in the window. It was beautiful.

"Is it time to play dreidel yet?" asked David.

"Sure!" said his dad. He brought out a wooden top and a bag of peanuts to pass around to the players.

22

"It's easy to play," David told Michael. "I'll show you how." He sat next to Michael and explained what to do. It was an exciting game. At first it looked like David's grandpa would win all the peanuts, but then Michael got lucky and won the game.

After a few more games of dreidel, it was time to pass out gifts. "In our family, we give small gifts on the first seven nights of Hanukkah and a bigger gift on the last night," said David's dad.

"First, here's a little something for all of the children," said David's grandpa. He gave each of them a handful of gold coins.

"Is this a special kind of money?" asked Michael.

"It sure is," said David. "It's chocolate! You have to peel off the gold foil."

Then David and his sister and cousin opened their gifts. David got a pick-up truck, his sister got a doll, and his cousin got a firetruck.

By now, it was time for Michael to go home. He thanked David's mother for the dinner, and he thanked David for sharing Hanukkah.

"Before you go, I have a gift for you," said David. Michael opened the little red box. Inside was a wooden dreidel.

"Wow, my own dreidel! Thanks!" said Michael. "I can't wait to tell my mom and dad all about tonight. Good night, everyone. Happy Hanukkah!"

More About Hanukkah

The Game of Dreidel

Dreidel is a favorite Hanukkah game. The top used has a special meaning. The marks on the four sides of the top are letters in the Hebrew language. They are the first letters in the message, "A great miracle happened there." Dreidel is simple to play, once you get the hang of it. Here are the rules:

1. To start, each player gets the same number (usually 10-15) of peanuts, raisins, pennies, or whatever object is chosen to play with.

2. Each player puts one peanut (for example) into the center of the playing area. The peanuts in the middle are called the pot.

3. Players take turns spinning the dreidel. The letter that lands facing up tells the player what to do:

(nun): The player does nothing.

(gimmel): The player takes the whole pot. Then everyone puts another peanut in before the next player spins.

(heh): The player takes half of the pot.

(shin): The player puts one peanut in the pot.

4. Whenever the pot is empty or there is just one peanut left, everyone puts in one before the next player spins.

5. The winner is the player who ends up with all of the peanuts when everyone else has lost.

Make Your Own Dreidel

There are many different kinds of dreidels. Here is a simple one that you can make. You will need:

- a small piece of heavy cardboard
- scissors
- a ruler
- a pen or markers
- a short pencil, about 3 inches long

1. Cut a square from the cardboard. Each side should be about 2 or 3 inches. (Make sure all sides are equal.)

2. Connect the corners by drawing an X in the middle of the square, as shown.

3. Draw the letters in each section, as shown.

4. Carefully poke a hole in the middle of the X with one blade of the scissors. Poke the pencil through the hole. Practice spinning your dreidel. (You may have to move the pencil up or down to make it spin well.)

1.

2.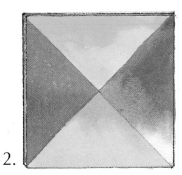

3.

4.

Star of David Mobile

The Star of David is an important Jewish symbol. It can also be a pretty Hanukkah decoration! Here's how you can make a Star of David mobile:

You will need:

—six pipe cleaners (preferably white)
—glue
—glitter (preferably silver or blue)
—white thread

1. Form a triangle with three pipe cleaners. Twist the ends to hold the triangle together. Do the same with the other three pipe cleaners.

2. Place one triangle upside-down over the other triangle to form a six-sided star. Where the two triangles touch each other, tie the pipe cleaners together with thread as shown.

3. Decorate the Star of David by gluing glitter to the pipe cleaners. When the glue is completely dry, use a loop of thread to hang your Star of David mobile.

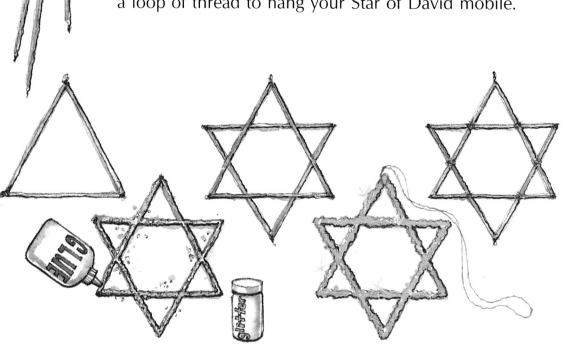

The Dreidel Song

   While you play dreidel, you can sing the dreidel song! It may help you remember the rules.

Oh, dreidel, dreidel, dreidel,
I made it out of clay.
And when my dreidel's ready,
Oh, dreidel I will play!
I'll take my little dreidel
And give it a good strong spin.
I hope it lands on Gimmel,
For then I'm sure to win.
If I spin Heh, I take half,
But none if I spin Nun.
I get the pot with Gimmel
With Shin I must pay one.

The Jewish Calendar

   Sometimes Hanukkah comes in November, and sometimes it comes in December. But it always begins on the same day in the Jewish calendar. The Jewish calendar has different months from the calendar you are used to. Hanukkah always begins on the twenty-fifth day of the Jewish month named Kislev.

Hanukkah or Chanukah?

   Hanukkah is spelled many different ways in English, and no way is right or wrong. That's because Hanukkah is a word from the Hebrew language. Hebrew has different letters from the English language (remember the letters on the dreidel?), so people try to spell it as it sounds.